BEN M. BAGLIO

The Curious Kitten

Illustrated by
Andy Ellis

A
LITTLE APPLE
PAPERBACK

SCHOLASTIC INC.
New York   Toronto   London   Auckland   Sydney
Mexico City   New Delhi   Hong Kong   Buenos Aires

ISBN 0-439-41915-8

12 11 10 9 8 7 6 5 4 3 2   2 3 4 5 6 7/0

Printed in the U.S.A.   40
First Scholastic printing, November 2002

To Sufi — another very curious puss!

Special thanks to Narinder Dhami

1

"Mom, where do tigers live?" Mandy Hope asked. She was pasting a picture of a tiger into her animal scrapbook.

It was the first day of winter vacation and almost time for morning office hours at the Animal Ark clinic. Mandy's mom and dad were vets. The clinic where they worked was built onto the back of their cottage. Mandy loved that. There were always plenty of animals around!

Emily Hope looked up from the pile of letters she was opening. "Well, there are tigers in Russia and some in China — but India has the most tigers," she said. "They live in the jungle."

Mandy pressed the picture down carefully on the next blank page. "I'd *love* to go to India and see the tigers!" She sighed.

Her mom smiled. "One day, we'll go," she promised. "Your scrapbook's getting very full. We'll buy a new one when we go shopping."

"Great!" Mandy said happily.

She had collected *lots* of pictures.
She might even need *two* new
scrapbooks!

"Mandy?"

Mandy looked around.

Jean Knox, the Animal Ark
receptionist, had come into the
kitchen.

"There's someone in the waiting room asking for you," Jean said, her eyes twinkling.

"Who?" Mandy asked, jumping up.

"Your friend Jill Redfern," said Jean.

Mandy rushed into the Animal Ark waiting room. It was very crowded. It always was on a Monday morning!

She spotted Jill sitting in the corner. Her friend was with a woman holding a large cat carrier.

"Hi, Mandy," Jill said, waving

4

at her. "This is my aunt. She's brought her kitten in to get a microchip!"

"Hello, Mandy," Jill's aunt said, smiling. "I'm Sarah — and this is Shamrock."

Mandy smiled back, then
went over and peered into the cat
carrier. Inside was a tabby kitten.

He had a fluffy golden brown
coat, striped with black — just like
a tiger! He was *very* cute.

"Hello, Shamrock!" Mandy said. Then she looked at Sarah. "He's gorgeous! But why have you named him Shamrock?" she asked.

Sarah smiled. "Look at his eyes," she said.

Mandy pushed her fingers through the wire. The kitten began to purr and rubbed his head against Mandy's hand. Then he looked up at her with the greenest eyes Mandy had ever seen! As green as shamrock leaves.

Mandy grinned. "Good name!" she agreed. She laughed as Shamrock poked a fluffy paw through the wire and tried to grab the sleeve of her sweatshirt.

"You told me all about microchips, Mandy, remember?" asked Jill.

Mandy nodded. Microchips helped owners find their pets when they were lost.

"Once Shamrock's chip is fitted, I'm going to let him out into the yard," Sarah said. "I've taken the week off from work so that I can watch him. He might be a little scared out there at first."

Just then, Mandy's dad, Adam Hope, looked into the waiting room and smiled. "I'm ready for Shamrock Redfern now," he said.

Mandy grinned. Shamrock was trying to open the latch on

the carrier, pulling at it with his teeth as hard as he could. "And I think Shamrock's ready for *you*, Dad!"

2

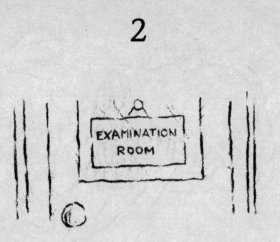

"Dad, can I come in and watch, please?" Mandy asked, as Sarah carried Shamrock into the examination room.

Dr. Adam looked at Sarah.

Sarah smiled. "Of course," she said.

"He seems to be a lively little fellow!" Dr. Adam grinned as Shamrock tried again to pull the carrier door open. "Let's let him out."

Mandy watched as her father undid the latch. Sometimes cats and kittens didn't want to come out onto the examining table. But right away, Shamrock jumped out, looking around. Then he

skidded toward the edge of the table, ready to explore.

"Oh, no, you don't," said Dr. Adam, grasping the kitten firmly.

Shamrock gave an unhappy meow. He looked up at Dr. Adam with his big green eyes, as if to say, *"Spoilsport!"*

Mandy and Jill burst out laughing.

"He's into *everything*," Sarah said. "He's been in every cupboard in my house and climbed up every curtain. He's just so nosy! And he's *always* trying to pull his collar and name tag off!"

"Then it's a very good idea for him to have a microchip before he goes outside," Dr. Adam said. He grinned as Shamrock tried to burrow up the sleeve of his white coat. "Just in case he forgets his way home!"

"Dad, I think Shamrock's got his head stuck!" Mandy pointed out. Shamrock was struggling to get out of Dr. Adam's sleeve and meowing for help.

Dr. Adam laughed and rescued Shamrock. He handed the kitten to Sarah, then sorted through his equipment. "We use a needle to put the microchip in Shamrock's neck," he said.

"But it doesn't hurt," Mandy added, seeing that Sarah and Jill looked a little

worried. She'd watched her dad fit a tiny chip under a pet's skin before.

Her dad nodded. "Shamrock won't even know it's there," he said.

"So how does the microchip help find Shamrock if he gets lost?" Jill asked.

"The microchip has a number on it," Dr. Adam said. "And the number is stored in a computer, with Sarah's address and phone number. So if someone finds Shamrock, a vet can use a special machine to read the number on his microchip and find out who his owner is."

"That's great!" Sarah said. "But I'm still a little worried about letting Shamrock outside. What if he runs off?"

"Well, when he goes out into the yard, make sure that he's hungry," Dr. Adam said. He prepared the needle. "Most kittens won't stray too far away from their next meal."

"Good idea!" said Sarah, looking happier. "Shamrock

is always hungry. He uses up so much energy exploring everywhere!"

Jill turned to Mandy. "Would you like to come home with us and watch Shamrock go outside for the very first time?" she asked.

Mandy's face lit up. "I'd love to!" She beamed, tickling Shamrock's fat little tummy.

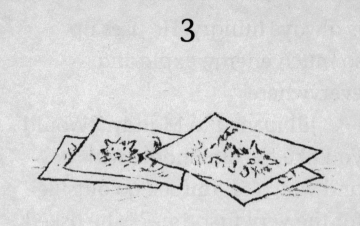

3

"You're home, Shamrock," Mandy said as she carried the kitten up to Sarah's front door. She and Jill had taken turns carrying the carrier during the walk through Welford. "You'll soon be free again!"

Shamrock meowed loudly and pawed crossly at the sides of the carrier.

"He can't wait to get out!" Jill grinned. "Maybe he's hungry."

"He wants to get out and have a good look around, you mean!" Sarah said, unlocking the door.

They all went into the kitchen.

Mandy put the cat carrier down on the floor. "Should I let Shamrock out?" she asked.

Sarah nodded. "I'll find some string," she said.

As soon as Mandy opened the carrier, Shamrock jumped out.

He rushed over to her and Jill, purring loudly as they ruffled his fur. But after a few seconds he dashed off again.

"Where's he going?" Jill asked.

"Look!" Mandy pointed across the kitchen. The door of Sarah's washing machine was open, and Shamrock was standing on his back legs, peering inside.

Mandy rushed over and grabbed the kitten just as he was about to jump in. "You're clean enough already, Shamrock." She laughed. The kitten didn't seem to agree. He sat down on the floor and began to wash himself with his tiny pink tongue.

Sarah sighed. "I'd better keep that door closed from now on," she said. Then she looked at her watch. "It's not quite time to take Shamrock out yet. Let's have a snack while we're waiting."

Mandy and Jill nodded.

"OK. Can I show Mandy the photos of Shamrock when he was really tiny, Aunt Sarah?" Jill asked.

Sarah smiled. "Sure," she

said. "The album is next to
the TV."

Jill and Mandy went off with
their orange juice and chocolate
cookies to find it.

In the photos, Mandy saw
that Shamrock was fluffier when
he was a tiny kitten. But his coat
was more tiger-stripy now. And
she liked tiger stripes!

Afterward, Mandy and Jill went to look for Shamrock. They found him in the kitchen. He'd finished washing himself and was sitting by his food bowl.

Sarah looked at her watch again and smiled. "Now it's time for Shamrock's next meal — and his rumbling tummy knows it!" she said.

She picked up the kitten and opened the back door. "All right, girls," she said. "Time to take him outside!"

Mandy looked around the backyard. It wasn't very big, so there weren't many places for Shamrock to hide. And the fences were too high for a kitten to jump over. There were no holes in them, either, for Shamrock to get through. *He will be really safe,* she thought.

Shamrock was looking around, too. He sniffed the air hard, and his eyes darted everywhere.

"Well, here goes!" said Sarah, sounding a little nervous. She put

Shamrock gently down on the grass.

Mandy watched the kitten as he looked around his big new world.

Shamrock took a few careful steps over the lawn. A butterfly fluttered over his head, and he snapped playfully at it. Then he looked at Mandy and the others as if to say, *"Aren't I clever?"*

They all laughed, and
Shamrock raced back to them,
purring. He skidded to a halt, and
then pounced on one of Mandy's
shoelaces.

"Shamrock!" Sarah said,
pretending to be cross.

The kitten ran off, tail waving
wildly. He ran as far as he
could — until he reached the end
of the lawn, when he was stopped
by some bushes. Then he ran
across the grass in the other
direction — until the fence
stopped him again.

"He doesn't seem at all scared
of being outside," Mandy said.

"He loves it!" Jill laughed.
Shamrock chased after a leaf that

was dancing in the breeze. "Clever boy, Shamrock!" she called.

They watched Shamrock explore the yard for a long time. He was having great fun. But every so often, he'd come bouncing back for a stroke and a cuddle.

"I think he's making sure we haven't left him on his own," Mandy said, grinning. She picked up Shamrock and he purred loudly.

"I'm so pleased that he's coming back to us and not trying to run off!" Sarah said. She seemed less worried now.

Before long, the kitten began to struggle in Mandy's arms. He

wanted to get down again. Mandy
put Shamrock back on the grass,
and he bounded across the lawn,
pouncing on daisies as he went.

Mandy beamed. The kitten
was really enjoying himself!

Suddenly, a blackbird flew
overhead. It landed in one of the
trees next to the fence.

Shamrock spotted it right away. He raced over and was up the trunk in a flash, digging his sharp little claws into the bark. The blackbird flew off in alarm.

"Shamrock!" Sarah called. "Come down!"

The kitten
wasn't listening.
He was climbing
farther up the tree.
A second later, he
was level with the
top of the fence.

Mandy gasped.
"He won't jump
over, will he?" she
said anxiously.

"No, it's much
too high," Sarah
said.

But Shamrock
didn't seem to
think so. He
crawled out onto

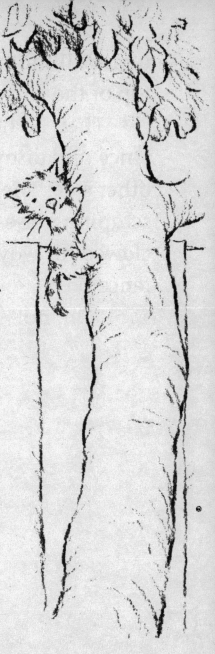

a branch that was level with the top of the fence.

Then he hopped onto the fence and disappeared over the other side. There was a loud scraping noise as the kitten clawed his way down the wooden fence post.

"Oh, no!" Mandy cried.

4

They all rushed over to the back gate.

Then Sarah groaned. "I forgot — it's locked!" she cried. "I'll get the key!" She raced back inside.

Mandy's heart thumped. Jill looked worried, too.

Suddenly, Mandy remembered what her dad had said. "Food!"

she yelled. "Sarah — he might come back for food!"

Sarah rushed back out into the yard. She had a key in one hand and a box of dry kitten food in the other. Quickly, she unlocked the gate, and they all rushed through.

They were in an alley. It ran behind the yards, then led out into the street in front of Sarah's house. But there was no sign of Shamrock.

Mandy's heart sank. If Shamrock had run out into the street, she just hoped he had stayed away from the traffic.

They ran to the end of the alley.

"Shamrock! Come here, boy!"

Sarah called. She shook the box of dry food loudly.

But there was no sign of the kitten.

Mandy sighed. Even a rumbling tummy wasn't going to stop *this* curious kitten's adventure.

Peter Foster was walking by with his dad. Peter was in Mandy and Jill's class. He was walking his cairn terrier pup, Timmy.

"Hi, Peter," Mandy said. She bent down to give Timmy a quick pat. The pup wagged his tail hard, then jumped up and licked Mandy's chin.

Mandy looked up at Peter.

"We're looking for a tabby kitten," she said.

"You haven't seen one out here, have you, Peter?" Jill added.

"Sorry, no," Peter said. "And Timmy would have noticed a kitten running around. He tries to chase cats, I'm afraid!"

Peter and his dad wished them luck. They walked off with Timmy toward the village green.

"At least Shamrock's got his microchip," Mandy said. "*And* the name tag on his collar."

Jill looked a little more cheerful. "You're right, Mandy," she agreed.

"Should we search the front yards in the street?" Mandy asked.

"Yes," said Sarah. "You two go one way, and I'll go the other." She looked very worried. "But don't cross the road, even if you see Shamrock on the other side," she warned. "Come and find me."

Mandy and Jill nodded, then set off down the street. They stopped at every gate and peered in. They just *had* to find Shamrock.

Then a flash of bright yellow in one of the yards caught Mandy's eye. Something was hooked over one of the branches of a large, leafy bush.

She went over to see what it was. "It's Shamrock's collar!" she gasped.

Jill rushed to
see. She nodded,
her eyes wide.
"It's definitely
Shamrock's.
That's Aunt Sarah's
phone number
on the name tag,"
she said. "It'll be even harder
to find him now!"

"Thank goodness he has his
microchip," Mandy said.

Jill ran to get her aunt, and
the three of them searched the
area where Mandy had found the
collar. Sarah kept on shaking
the box of dry food loudly.

They asked everyone they

met if they'd seen Shamrock.
But they didn't find the missing
kitten.

"Where *can* he be?" Jill said
tearfully as they all stood outside
Sarah's house, not knowing where
else to look.

Just then, the Animal Ark Land Rover turned into the street.

"Here's my mom," Mandy said in a small voice. "It's time for me to go home."

Dr. Emily pulled up at the curb and climbed out. The smile on her face faded as she saw all the gloomy faces. "What on earth has happened?" she asked.

"Oh, Mom!" Mandy said in a wobbly voice. "Shamrock's disappeared, and no one knows *where* he is!"

5

"Cheer up, dear," Dr. Emily said, putting an arm around Mandy and giving her a hug.

Mandy and her mom were sitting in the Animal Ark living room watching TV, while her dad worked the evening shift at the clinic. Mandy hadn't eaten much of her supper. She'd been too upset about Shamrock.

"I bet someone will find

Shamrock and take him to the local animal shelter," Dr. Emily added. "And he has a microchip now."

Mandy nodded. But it was getting dark. She couldn't bear to think of the little kitten out there, all on his own. Sarah had said she would telephone them as soon as Shamrock turned up. But the phone hadn't rung at all.

"Why don't you go and see what Dad is doing?" her mom said. "Seeing some other animals might stop you from worrying for a while."

"OK," Mandy said. She gave her mom a little smile and went through into the Animal Ark waiting room.

There was hardly anyone left there. Jean Knox was busy at her desk. A girl carrying a gray rabbit in a cage was paying her bill. The only other person was a young man with a cardboard box on his lap.

Mandy could see that it

wasn't a regular
carrying case,
just an old
supermarket
box with holes
punched in
the lid.

The man
saw Mandy
looking, and
grinned at her. "Hi, there."

"Hello," Mandy said shyly.
"What's in there?"

"A kitten," the man replied.
The sound of loud scratching
came from inside the box.

"Oh," Mandy said sadly,
thinking of Shamrock. "What's
wrong with it?"

The young man shrugged. "Well, nothing, as far as I know," he said. "I found it in my yard, eating some bacon rinds I'd put out for the birds. I didn't know where else to take it. It's not wearing a collar, so I'm hoping the vet can check for a microchip."

Mandy's eyes opened wide, and her heart beat faster. "Could I have a look, please?" she asked.

The young man nodded and opened up the cardboard flaps. A fluffy golden brown head, striped with black, popped out.

"Meow!" the kitten said crossly.

"Shamrock!" Mandy cried.

She scooped up the kitten and hugged him hard. Shamrock rubbed his face against Mandy's and began to purr happily.

"Oh, Shamrock!" Mandy whispered. "You're safe!"

She looked at the young man, who seemed surprised. Then she laughed. "You're right," she said. "My dad *can* check for a microchip — but there's no need to this time. *I* can tell you who this kitten belongs to!"

6

"Hello?"

Mandy's heart beat faster when she heard Jill's voice at the other end of the line. "Jill, it's Mandy!" she cried. "I've found Shamrock!"

"What?" Jill gasped. "Aunt Sarah, Mandy's found Shamrock!"

"Oh, thank goodness!"

Mandy could hear Sarah hurrying down the hall.

"Where did she find him? Is he all right?"

Mandy grinned. She was still holding Shamrock, who was trying to jump down and explore the waiting room. "He's fine," she said. Then she explained exactly how the runaway kitten had been found.

"We'll be over to pick up Shamrock right away," Sarah said, taking the phone from her niece. "And can you keep the person who found him there, so that we can say thank you?"

"OK," Mandy said happily.

She put down the phone. Her mom and dad had both come out to the waiting room to see what was going on. They were talking to the young man who'd brought Shamrock in, and smiling. "Sarah and Jill are on their way," Mandy told them. She turned to the man. "And they'd like you to wait, so that they can thank you."

The man looked a little embarrassed. "I ought to be getting home —" he began.

Dr. Emily shook her head firmly. "Jill and her aunt will want to thank you properly, Mr. . . ."

"Smith," the man said. "But call me Jonathan."

"Yes, you really must stay, Jonathan," agreed Dr. Adam. "If it wasn't for you, Shamrock might still be lost! Come into the kitchen for a cup of tea while we wait."

*   *   *

"I wonder if this tiny fellow *is* microchipped," Jonathan said, as he sat in the Animal Ark kitchen. Shamrock had jumped onto his lap and was having his tummy tickled. "He certainly *should* be if he's so curious!"

Dr. Adam nodded and grinned. "The little rascal was microchipped just this morning. I did it myself!"

"So you must like it here, Shamrock," Jonathan joked. "Two visits in one day!"

Shamrock then began to struggle to get down to do more exploring. He disappeared under the kitchen table.

"Get the cookie jar, would you, dear?" Dr. Adam said to Mandy.

Mandy nodded. When she came back from the pantry with the jar, she took a bite from a chocolate-chip cookie. Then she crawled under the table to see what Shamrock was up to.

But there was no sign of him. "Shamrock!" she called. "Where have you gone this time?"

"I hope he hasn't gotten lost again," Jonathan said, as he sipped his tea.

"He can't be far away," said Mandy.

Just then, the doorbell rang. Mandy put her half-eaten cookie on the table and raced to the door. "Here they are!" she yelled.

Jill and her aunt were standing outside, beaming.

"Where's that naughty kitten of mine?" Sarah asked.

"In the kitchen," Mandy

replied. "But we're not sure exactly where," she said under her breath.

Sarah and Jill followed Mandy back into the kitchen.

After smiling hello to Dr. Adam and Dr. Emily, Sarah

turned to Jonathan. "Thank you *so* much for bringing Shamrock here. It was certainly the right place!" she said happily.

"It was no trouble — you're welcome," said Jonathan, smiling back.

Sarah looked around. "So, where is he?" she asked.

Dr. Adam coughed. "Er, he's here *somewhere*," he said. "He's gone off exploring again." Everyone laughed.

Suddenly, a scrabbling noise made them jump. A moment later, Shamrock squeezed out from behind the stove, looking somewhat dirty and dusty and meowing at the top of his voice.

"Shamrock!" Sarah quickly scooped him up. "You bad, bad boy!" she said, giving him a hug.

"He must have come out to see why we're all laughing," Mandy said, scratching the top of Shamrock's furry head. "Shamrock, you really are a curious kitten!"

Shamrock meowed loudly, as if he really agreed.